# EVELYN DEL REY

## IS MOVING AWAY

To Kate Fletcher, who always helps me
find the way to the heart of a child's story
MM

For my friend Tania. Although I no longer see you each day,
I have you in my heart. You are my friend and my treasure.
SS

Text copyright © 2020 by Meg Medina
Illustrations copyright © 2020 by Sonia Sánchez

First edition 2020

Library of Congress Catalog Card Number 2020912752
ISBN 978-1-5362-0704-0

20 21 22 23 24 25 CCP 10 9 8 7 6 5 4 3

Printed in Shenzhen, Guangdong, China

This book was typeset in Avenir.
The illustrations were created digitally.

Candlewick Press
99 Dover Street
Somerville, Massachusetts 02144

www.candlewick.com

# EVELYN DEL REY
## IS MOVING AWAY

Meg Medina

*illustrated by* **Sonia Sánchez**

CANDLEWICK PRESS

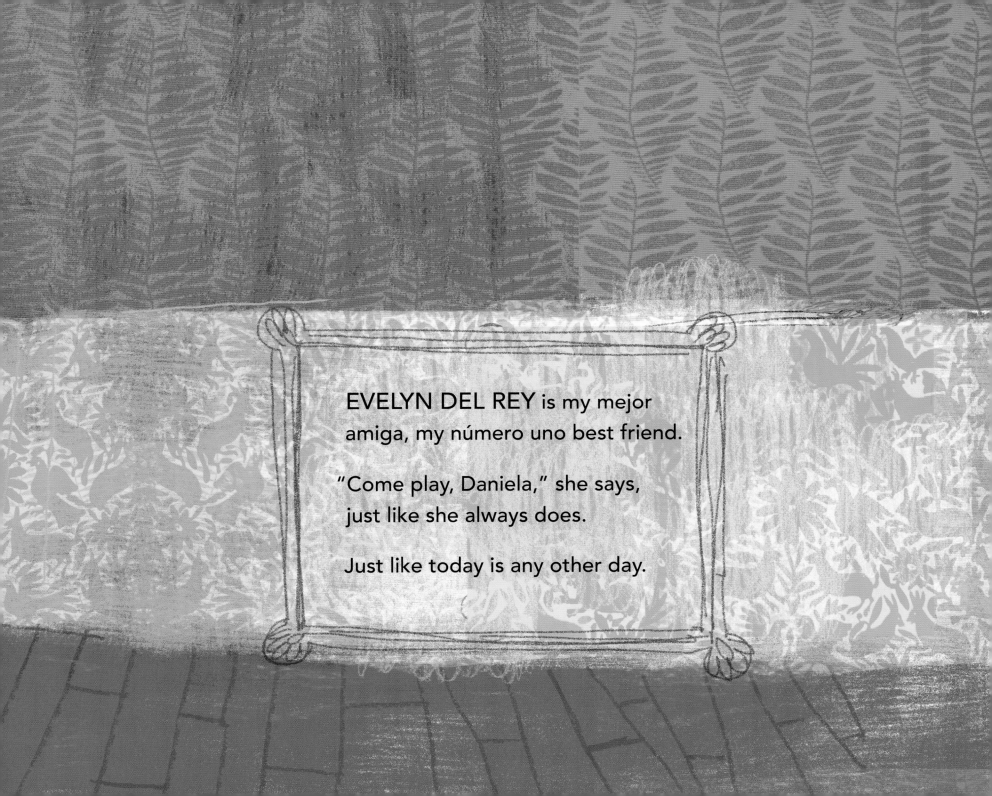

EVELYN DEL REY is my mejor amiga, my número uno best friend.

"Come play, Daniela," she says, just like she always does.

Just like today is any other day.

So I bundle up and cross the street.
A big truck with its mouth wide open is
parked at the curb, ready to gobble up
Evelyn's mirror with the stickers around
the edge, her easel for painting on rainy
days, and the sofa that we bounce on to
get to the moon.

She is waiting for me
inside the iron doors.

Then we climb the steps
two at a time,
just like we always do.

We sneak past grouchy Mr. Miller's door and wave to Mr. Soo, who's feeding pigeons from the hall window.

Señora Flores gives us each a cookie and says, "It's the big day!" when we walk by.

Our apartments are almost twins, just like us. That's why I already knew all the good places for hide-and-seek, and the spot behind the heater where we keep our special finds.

But the walls in Evelyn's room are sunny yellow, while mine are pink like cotton candy.

And I live with my mami and a hamster, and she has a mami, a papi, and a cat.

We are mostly the same,
just like our apartments.

But not after today.

We find a still-empty box near the door. In no time,
I am a bus driver steering us all over the city. We play
until the tables that were bus stops are gone and the
beds that were skyscrapers have vanished, too.

When we look around, everything has disappeared
except us.

Soon the truck outside rumbles off, and there is a knock on the door.

"Hide!" we say, giggling. Just like we always do.

But our mothers see us before we can slip away. "Time to go," Mami says.

Evelyn and I hold hands in that wide empty space.
We lean back and start to spin in circles,
faster and faster, until everything is a blur around us.
Our fingers slip, but we don't let go until we wobble to the floor.

"We can talk every day after school," I tell her,
 though the world is still whirling.
"And you can visit me this summer," she says.
"And spend the night!"

But I know that tomorrow
everything will be different.

Evelyn will be in a new home
that doesn't match mine.

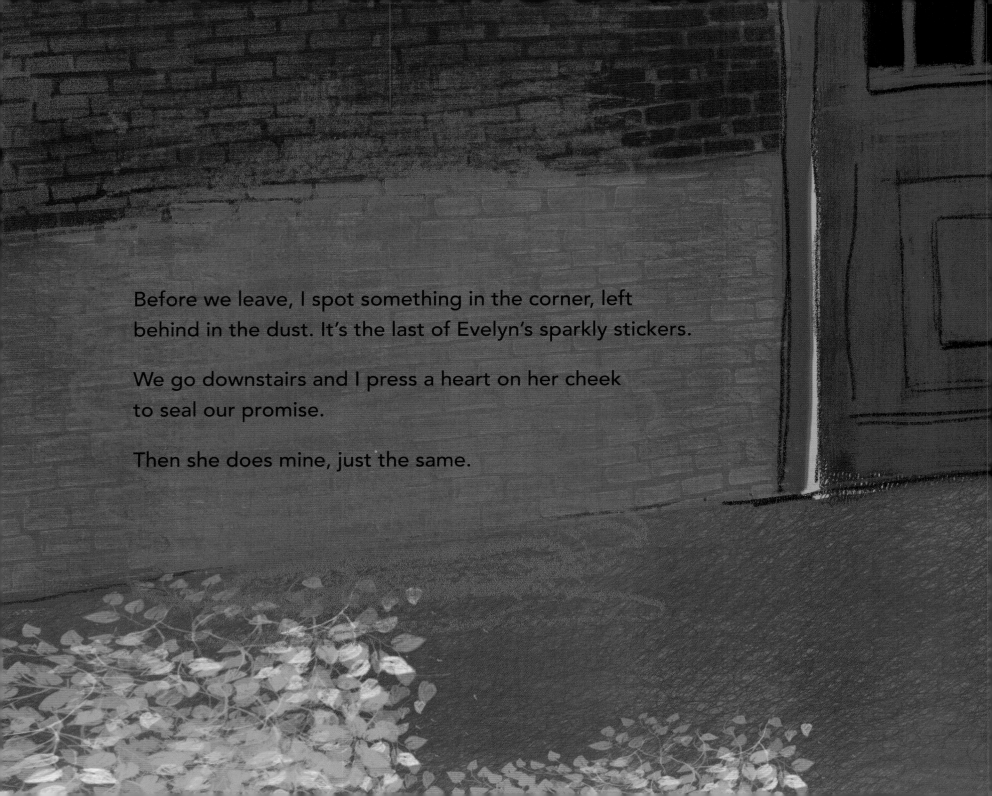

Before we leave, I spot something in the corner, left
behind in the dust. It's the last of Evelyn's sparkly stickers.

We go downstairs and I press a heart on her cheek
to seal our promise.

Then she does mine, just the same.

We say "¡Patata!" while Mami takes a photo.
We do our secret handshake one more time.

And then Evelyn hugs me hard.

Evelyn Del Rey is moving away.
So she won't be right here anymore.

Mami says not to be sad,
that we will both make new friends.

But when Evelyn waves one last time,
the stickers still on her cheeks,
I know she will always be my first mejor amiga,
my número uno best friend . . .

the one I will always know by heart.